How to Write a Bestselling Mafia Romance

Just Bae

Contents

Introduction

As you stand on the threshold of mastering the art of writing mafia romance, you're not just beginning a creative endeavor; you're embarking on a journey to uncover the secrets behind crafting narratives that captivate readers and dominate bestseller lists. Mafia romance novels, with their intoxicating blend of danger, passion, and forbidden love, offer a unique challenge and opportunity for writers. This book is designed to be your roadmap, guiding you through the intricacies of creating a story that thrives on the edge of society's boundaries, where every whispered secret holds power and every forbidden touch challenges the status quo.

Drawing inspiration from the timeless themes of star-crossed lovers and tumultuous passions found in classics like "Romeo and Juliet" and "Wuthering Heights," we bridge the gap between the enduring allure of forbidden love and the shadowy dynamics of the mafia underworld. The essence of a bestselling mafia romance lies in its ability to weave these themes into a narrative where love doesn't just battle against external forces but flourishes amidst the danger and moral ambiguity of organized crime. The stakes are elevated, the emotions intensified, and the romance all the more exhilarating.

This guide aims to demystify the process of writing a mafia romance that resonates deeply with readers, blending the thrill of suspense with the depth of heartfelt connections. We delve into the psychology that draws readers into this world—a world where love is a rebellion, and every act of defiance is a testament to the human spirit. By combining action-packed suspense with profound emotional story-telling, we'll show you how to create a narrative that is both compelling and emotionally resonant.

As your mentor through the shadowy paths of mafia romance writing, our goal is to equip you with the tools necessary for crafting a narrative that not only enthralls readers but also cements your place among the ranks of bestselling authors. From developing characters that readers will root for to creating a setting that pulsates with life, from constructing plots rife with tension to writing scenes that simmer with intensity—every chapter of this book is a step toward realizing your potential as a mafia romance novelist.

We begin with an exploration of the historical origins and literary influences that have shaped the genre, providing a foundation upon which to build your stories. Understanding the evolution of mafia romance from its inception to its current status as a genre powerhouse will inspire your writing, ensuring authenticity and depth.

Through this book, we'll guide you on how to harness the elements that make mafia romance irresistible—the mix of danger, the dynamics of power, and the allure of the forbidden. By weaving these elements into your stories, you can create narratives that not only captivate but leave a lasting impression on your audience.

Embarking on this journey, you'll learn to navigate the themes and tropes that define mafia romance, from loyalty and betrayal to redemption arcs that add complexity and resolution to your characters' journeys. Mastering these elements will enable you to craft stories that thrill and move your readers in equal measure.

In the realm of mafia romance, character development is key to forging a connection with your audience. We'll guide you in creating protagonists and antagonists who are relatable, flawed yet redeemable, strong yet vulnerable—characters whose journeys reflect the intricacies of the mafia world and resonate with readers on a personal level.

Let this introduction be the first step toward your goal of writing a bestselling mafia romance. With this guide as your companion, you're not just learning to write; you're on the path to creating a masterpiece that will captivate the hearts of readers and leave an indelible mark on the genre.

Preface

As you venture into the enigmatic world of mafia romance, prepare to immerse yourself in a realm where high stakes and intense passions rule the lives of its characters. This journey transcends ordinary romantic fiction, inviting you to explore a narrative landscape where emotions amplify against a backdrop of ever-present danger, and each love story deepens with the intensity of forbidden desires. You're on the cusp of delving into a genre that daringly crosses the boundaries of conventional romance, venturing into the raw and untamed territories of the outlawed.

Mafia romance, celebrated for its heady mix of peril, passion, and taboo love, carves a distinctive niche in the broad spectrum of romantic literature. It flourishes on the edge of societal norms, in realms where lawlessness intertwines with an innate human yearning for connection and love. The excitement of navigating a universe defined by unique codes and allegiances lends unparalleled depth to the romantic ventures it hosts.

Picture yourself at the frontier of this world, where moral lines blur, and love contends against all odds—not only societal or familial obstacles but against the very laws that structure society. In mafia romance, your characters are embroiled not just in a quest for love but in battles for survival, power, and redemption. Their struggles lend every instance of tenderness, every whisper of affection, a preciousness born of peril.

The genre's magic lies in its capacity to oscillate between the darkest and most tender extremes of human experience. The inherent dangers of the mafia lifestyle elevate emotional stakes, imbuing every choice, risk, and sacrifice with a gravity that intoxicates both reader and character alike. The allure of the forbidden, the adrenaline of a world veiled in secrets and betrayals, lays the groundwork for love stories that are endured rather than merely lived.

Mafia romance challenges its characters—and, vicariously, its readers—to navigate the intricacies of love in a world brimming with consequences. Here, heart loyalty may clash with familial or organizational ties. The genre dissects power, control, and autonomy's nuances, not only within criminal enterprises but also within the hearts that dare to love amid these confines.

The passion encapsulated within these pages isn't safe or predictable; it's a consuming wildfire, fueled by the intensity of forbidden desires and the desperation of lovers cognizant that every shared moment might be their last. This is mafia romance's essence: a love fierce, desperate, and unyielding, set against a backdrop equally relentless.

As you delve into writing mafia romance, you'll discover that this genre transcends mere love stories against a criminal backdrop. It stands as a testament to love's enduring triumph over the gravest dangers, celebrating the human spirit's resilience when tested by ultimate loyalty and sacrifice challenges. You are not merely traversing a genre; you are entering a realm where every heartbeat is a defiance, every touch a treasure, and every love story a testament to the human heart's indomitable strength.

Welcome to the world of mafia romance, where danger and desire intertwine, and the path to a happy ending is fraught with peril yet illuminated by the fiercest passions. In this domain of shadows and whispered promises, where every breath is laced with danger and longing, the allure of mafia romance unfolds. It's a genre that embraces the darkness, inviting you to look deeper, to explore passions found only when love confronts the underworld's iron grip.

In the narratives of mafia romance, you're not just observing characters fall in love; you're accompanying them as they navigate the precarious terrains of crime, power, and allegiance. The stakes are unimaginable, where a single misstep could lead to more than heartbreak; it could be fatal. Yet, in this setting of danger and moral ambiguity, love's brightest flames ignite. This stark contrast, this play of light against darkness, renders the genre irresistibly captivating.

As you deepen your exploration, you'll encounter a genre as varied as it is enthralling. From raw, gritty tales of survival and dominance to poignant stories of redemption and sacrifice, the characters you'll meet embody the genre's richness; from the hardened mafia boss softened by love to the innocent ensnared in organized crime's vortex. Each character's journey challenges our perceptions of love, loyalty, and redemption.

The forbidden love at mafia romance's heart transcends societal taboos or superficial barriers; it's a love that flourishes in survival's essence. It's a love that chooses defiance not just against the odds but against a world that prioritizes power over the heart. This defiance, this depth of emotional journey, the complexity of choices faced by characters, and the intensity of their love set mafia romance apart.

Engaging with mafia romance, you sign up for an emotional rollercoaster. The tension lies not only in external threats, power battles, or clashes with rivals but in characters' internal struggles torn between worlds, between right and wrong, love and duty. The allure of the forbidden gains new dimensions here, where each shadowed moment is a triumph against fate.

Yet, it's not solely the genre's darkness and danger that define it; it's also the emergent light. Mafia romance stories are hope beacons, showcasing love's capacity to heal, redeem, and transform, illuminating even the darkest corners.

Standing at the threshold of this captivating world, you're poised to experience a genre that enthralls, challenges, and ultimately uplifts. Mafia romance is an ode to love's power to transcend life shrouded in secrecy and danger, a celebration of the fierce determination to love, protect, and fight for a love that defies all odds.

Welcome, then, to the intoxicating dance of mafia romance, where every step is laden with risk, every turn a potential betrayal, but the reward—a love that overcomes all—is infinitely worth every challenge. Here, in the genre's embrace, you'll find stories that captivate your imagination and touch your heart, leaving imprints that endure beyond the final page.

Prologue

The genre of mafia romance, a compelling fusion of romantic entanglements and the shadowy dynamics of organized crime, is not merely a product of contemporary fascination but a genre deeply rooted in historical and cultural developments. To understand its allure and complexity, it's essential to explore the intricate tapestry of its origins, tracing back to early literature, the cultural impact of organized crime, and the genre's evolution through the 20th and into the 21st century.

Literary Precursors and Cultural Fascination

The genesis of mafia romance can be traced back to literary explorations of crime and morality. Classic works such as "Crime and Punishment" and "Les Misérables" laid the groundwork for character-driven narratives that delve into the moral complexities of society's outcasts. These stories paved the way for a nuanced portrayal of characters who, though entangled with crime, exhibit a compelling depth and capacity for love and redemption.

The allure of the criminal underworld in literature expanded with the advent of hard-boiled detective stories in the early 20th century and noir fiction, where the lines between hero and villain blurred, setting a precedent for morally ambiguous protagonists who would become central to mafia romance narratives.

The Mafia in Historical Context

The real-world emergence of the Mafia, particularly the Sicilian Mafia and its American counterparts, played a pivotal role in shaping the genre's backdrop. The Mafia's code of honor, familial loyalty, and ruthless pursuit of power offered a rich narrative soil for stories of love and betrayal. The prohibition era, with its dramatic rise in organized crime, provided a historical backdrop that highlighted the mafia's influence in society, making it a symbol of rebellion against the stifling moral and legal constraints of the time.

Influence of Media and Popular Culture

The portrayal of the mafia in cinema and television during the 20th century significantly influenced public perception and fascination with organized crime. Films like "The Godfather" and series like "The Sopranos" painted a complex picture of mafia life, emphasizing themes of loyalty, family, and the pursuit of power, which resonated deeply with audiences. These portrayals contributed to the romanticization of the mafia lifestyle, setting the stage for the emergence of mafia romance as a genre that explores the tension between the criminal underworld and the pursuit of personal happiness and love.

Evolution of Mafia Romance as a Genre

Mafia romance emerged as a distinct genre towards the end of the 20th century, as writers began to focus on the romantic and erotic possibilities within the world of organized crime. Early mafia romance stories often featured male protagonists who were deeply involved in criminal activities, with female characters initially cast in roles that highlighted their vulnerability or innocence. Over time, the genre has evolved to include strong female protagonists who challenge traditional gender roles and engage with the complexities of power and autonomy within the mafia context.

Modern mafia romance novels explore a wide range of themes, including forbidden love, loyalty to family versus personal desires, and the moral dilemmas faced by characters embedded in the criminal underworld. The genre has expanded to include diverse settings beyond the traditional Sicilian or American mafia context, exploring organized crime in Russian, Irish, and other cultural backdrops and enriching the genre with a variety of cultural nuances and traditions.

Contemporary Developments and Themes

Today, mafia romance continues to captivate readers with stories that delve into the darkness of organized crime while illuminating the enduring power of love. Contemporary authors of the genre are increasingly focusing on character development, exploring the psychological depth of their protagonists, and challenging established norms and expectations. The genre has also seen a rise in diversity, with stories featuring a wider range of ethnic backgrounds, sexual orientations, and complex moral landscapes.

Themes of redemption, power dynamics, and the clash between personal desires and familial or organizational loyalty remain central to mafia romance, offering readers an escape into worlds where love defies the odds. The enduring appeal of the genre lies in its ability to blend the thrill of danger with the universal quest for connection, belonging, and love.

The Socio-Political Context

The Rise of the Mafia

The origin of the Mafia, particularly in Sicily in the 19th century, is intertwined with Sicily's tumultuous history of foreign domination and social upheaval. The Mafia initially emerged as a network of private enforcers and protectors in a society where the state was either absent or corrupt. This organization filled a power vacuum in Sicilian society, offering protection and enforcing justice according to its own codes, which were often in opposition to the formal law.

As Sicilian immigrants moved to the United States in the late 19th and early 20th centuries, they brought with them the familial and societal structures that had governed their lives in Sicily, including the Mafia. In the U.S., the Mafia found fertile ground in the prohibition era, engaging in bootlegging, gambling, and a range of other criminal activities. The American Mafia, or La Cosa Nostra, adapted and thrived, establishing a complex hierarchy and code of conduct that would capture the public's imagination for generations.

Cultural Fascination and Mythologization

The Mafia's rise to power and the public's fascination with its operations were significantly amplified by media portrayals. The Godfather novel by Mario Puzo, followed by Francis Ford Coppola's cinematic adaptation, played pivotal roles in mythologizing the Mafia, presenting it as an entity governed by honor and loyalty, despite its criminal undertakings. This romanticized view of the Mafia, highlighting themes of family, honor, and tragedy, has significantly influenced the development of mafia romance as a genre, blending the allure of forbidden love with the danger and moral ambiguity of the criminal underworld.

Literary Evolution

From Tragedy to Romance

The thematic elements central to mafia romance can be traced back to tragic literature and classic romantic narratives that explore forbidden love and the struggle against societal norms. Works such as "Romeo and Juliet" showcase the timeless appeal of love that defies familial and societal boundaries, a theme that resonates strongly in mafia romance narratives.

The 20th century saw the rise of gangster films and pulp fiction that featured the gritty realities of life within the Mafia, often focusing on the tragic fall of its members. These narratives laid the groundwork for a genre that would merge the thrilling aspects of life within organized crime with the deep emotional connections of romance.

Evolution of Romantic Fiction

Parallel to the development of crime and gangster narratives, the romance genre was evolving to explore increasingly diverse settings and complex characters. The late 20th century saw the rise of dark romance and romantic suspense, genres that blend the elements of danger, moral ambiguity, and passionate love. Mafia romance emerged from this confluence, offering narratives that combine the high stakes of life within the Mafia with the emotional depth and development characteristic of the romance genre.

Global Influence and Expansion

While the Italian Mafia and its American counterpart have been central to the development of the genre, mafia romance has expanded to include organized crime from various cultural backgrounds, including Russian Bratva, Irish Mob, and Japanese Yakuza. This diversification reflects a global fascination with the underworld's allure, adapting the core themes of mafia romance to different cultural contexts and legal landscapes.

Contemporary Resonance

Mafia romance continues to evolve, reflecting contemporary concerns and societal changes. Modern narratives often feature stronger, more independent characters, particularly heroines who challenge traditional gender roles within the patriarchal structure of organized crime. Themes of autonomy, power, and the quest for identity within the confines of the criminal underworld are explored in greater depth, resonating with a contemporary audience seeking narratives that reflect their complexities and contradictions.

Chapter 1

Unraveling the Mystery: Mafia Romance's Seductive Charm

The allure of mafia romance is a complex tapestry woven from threads of danger, power dynamics, forbidden desires, and the human psyche's deep-seated fascinations. As we peel back the layers of this enthralling genre, we uncover not just the narratives that hold readers captive but also the psychological underpinnings that make mafia romance irresistibly compelling. This exploration into the heart of the genre's appeal reveals why stories set against a backdrop of organized crime, with their tumultuous love affairs and moral quandaries, resonate so deeply with readers.

The Psychological Appeal of Mafia Romance

At its core, the appeal of mafia romance lies in its ability to tap into fundamental aspects of human psychology. These stories offer a narrative space where readers can explore their own desires, fears, and moral complexities from a safe distance. The genre provides a vicarious experience of the forbidden, allowing readers to indulge in the thrill of the taboo without real-world consequences. This psychological escapism is a key factor in the genre's popularity, offering an outlet for emotions and desires that are often suppressed or unexplored in daily life.

The Lure of the Forbidden

One of the most potent draws of mafia romance is the allure of the forbidden. The genre often portrays relationships and desires that defy societal norms and laws, echoing the age-old theme of forbidden love that has captivated audiences since the time of "Romeo and Juliet." This theme resonates with the intrinsic human desire to rebel against constraints, to explore the unknown, and to challenge the boundaries set by society. The forbidden nature of the love stories in mafia romance novels taps into the reader's yearning for adventure and the exploration of the self in relation to societal rules.

Danger and the Thrill of Survival

The omnipresent danger in mafia romance adds a thrilling dimension to the narrative, heightening the stakes of the romantic entanglement. This constant threat of violence and betrayal creates a backdrop of suspense that keeps readers on the edge of their seats. The psychological thrill of survival, of love in the face of deadly odds, speaks to the primal human instinct to seek safety and connection under threat. The genre's exploration of danger and survival resonates with the reader's own fears and desires, offering a cathartic experience where love triumphs over adversity.

Power Dynamics and Control

Mafia romance novels intricately explore power dynamics, both within the criminal underworld and the central romantic relationship. The genre delves into themes of dominance and submission, control and freedom, often blurring the lines between consensual and coercive power exchanges. This exploration of power speaks to the human fascination with control—both the desire to possess it and the fear of losing it. The complex power dynamics at play in mafia romance allow readers to explore aspects of dominance, submission, and autonomy in a context far removed from their everyday lives, providing a space to interrogate their own beliefs and desires related to power and control.

The Captivating Elements of Mafia Romance

The Enigma of the Mafia World

The secretive, often glamorous depiction of the mafia world offers readers an escape into a realm that is both dangerous and enticing. The allure of this closed, clandestine society is in its otherness, its deviation from the mundane realities of everyday life. The mafia world's enigmatic nature, with its codes of honor, loyalty, and its own brand of justice, fascinates readers, drawing them into a world that operates on the fringes of legality and morality.

Tumultuous Love Affairs

At the heart of mafia romance are the tumultuous love affairs that challenge and redefine the concept of love. These relationships are marked by intense passion, profound connections, and often, devastating obstacles. The depth and intensity of these love stories appeal to readers' desires for an all-consuming love that defies norms and overcomes insurmountable challenges. The emotional rollercoaster of these relationships, with their highs of passionate unity and lows of heart-wrenching conflict, offers readers an intense emotional experience that resonates with their deepest desires and fears about love.

The Quest for Redemption

Many mafia romance narratives center around the theme of redemption, whether through love, sacrifice, or personal transformation. This theme speaks to the universal human condition of flawedness and the desire for forgiveness and redemption. The genre's exploration of redemption through love offers a hopeful narrative that even the most hardened characters can find salvation in the strength and purity of their love. This quest for redemption resonates with readers' own hopes for transformation and the belief in the redemptive power of love.

Understanding the fascination behind mafia romance requires delving into the complex interplay between the genre's narrative elements and the psychological appeal they hold for readers. The allure of the forbidden, the thrill of danger, the exploration of power dynamics, and the enigmatic mafia world create a rich narrative tapestry that captivates readers. At the same time, the genre's exploration of tumultuous love affairs and the quest for redemption offers a deeply emotional experience that resonates with fundamental human desires and fears. Through this exploration, we gain insight into why mafia romance continues to enchant and engage readers, offering them an escape into a world where love, no matter how fraught with peril, remains the ultimate triumph.

Exploration of Identity and Morality

Mafia romance often places its characters—and, by extension, its readers—at the moral crossroads, challenging them to explore their own values and ethical boundaries. The genre's protagonists frequently grapple with questions of right and wrong, forced to make choices that blur the lines between justice and revenge, loyalty and betrayal. This moral ambiguity invites readers to question their own beliefs and the societal norms they adhere to. Through the characters' journeys, readers can explore aspects of their own identity and morality in a context that is removed from their everyday lives, providing a safe space to confront these complex issues.

The Role of Family and Loyalty

Central to the appeal of mafia romance is the emphasis on family and loyalty, themes that resonate on a universal level. The mafia's portrayal as a tight-knit community with a staunch code of honor and loyalty appeals to our innate desire for belonging and significance within a group. This portrayal taps into the psychological need for connection and the fear of isolation, drawing readers into a world where bonds of loyalty are often stronger than blood. The conflict between familial loyalty and romantic love adds a layer of tension to the narrative, compelling readers to navigate the delicate balance between individual desires and collective obligations. This exploration of loyalty and the sacrifices it entails speaks to the heart of the human condition, engaging readers on an emotional level that transcends the thrill of the criminal underworld.

The Dichotomy of Vulnerability and Strength

Mafia romance intricately explores the dichotomy between vulnerability and strength, particularly in its portrayal of love as both a weakness and a source of power. Characters in these stories often reveal their most vulnerable selves in the context of their romantic relationships, shedding the armor required by their life in the mafia. This vulnerability is juxtaposed with the strength drawn from love, illustrating how emotional openness can lead to personal empowerment. For readers, this exploration of vulnerability in a world defined by strength and power resonates with the universal struggle to reconcile one's own weaknesses with the desire to be seen as strong. It highlights the transformative power of love, not as a fairytale ideal but as a force that can bring even the most powerful to their knees and, paradoxically, lift them higher than ever before.

Catharsis and Emotional Release

Engaging with mafia romance provides a form of catharsis for readers, offering an emotional release through the vicarious experience of the characters' trials and triumphs. The genre's intense emotional conflicts, life-and-death stakes, and ultimate resolutions allow readers to process their own fears, desires, and unresolved conflicts in a controlled environment. This emotional journey through the narrative acts as a safe outlet for exploring personal anxieties and the universal quest for love and acceptance. The cathartic effect of mafia romance underscores the genre's psychological appeal, providing not just an escape from reality but a means of confronting and processing complex emotions.

Chapter 2

Forbidden Love: Recurring Themes in Mafia Romances

Mafia romance, a genre rich with complexity and depth, intertwines the visceral allure of danger with the raw power of emotional narratives. At the heart of its enduring appeal are the themes and tropes that resonate deeply with readers, drawing them into a world where love battles against a backdrop of crime and power. This chapter delves into the core themes of loyalty, betrayal, redemption, and sacrifice, and explores the popular tropes, including star-crossed lovers, redemption arcs, and the anti-hero, that define and distinguish mafia romance.

Common Themes in Mafia Romance

Loyalty

Loyalty, the backbone of any organized crime narrative, assumes a profound significance in mafia romance. It's a theme that tests characters' limits and loyalty not just to the family or organization but also to their own hearts. In these stories, loyalty often becomes a double-edged sword, posing dilemmas that challenge the protagonists' moral compasses and personal desires. The intricate dance between loyalty to the mafia's code and the loyalty owed to loved ones creates a fertile ground for conflict, driving the narrative towards critical junctures where characters must make life-altering decisions.

Betrayal

Hand in hand with loyalty is the theme of betrayal, which acts as a catalyst for many of the genre's most dramatic moments. Betrayal, whether real or perceived, shakes the foundations of trust and honor that the mafia world is built upon. It propels characters into situations where they must navigate the treacherous waters of revenge and forgiveness. The emotional depth of betrayal and its repercussions provide a rich narrative vein to explore, often leading characters to unexpected paths of personal growth and change.

Redemption

Redemption is a powerful theme in mafia romance, reflecting the genre's capacity to explore the nuances of human morality and the possibility of change. Characters in these stories are frequently flawed, having made choices that entangle them in a web of crime and violence. Redemption arcs offer them a path to atonement through love, sacrifice, or acts of courage that transcend their past misdeeds. This theme resonates deeply with readers, providing hope and reaffirming the belief in the transformative power of love and forgiveness.

Sacrifice

Sacrifice, a theme that often intersects with loyalty and redemption, is pivotal in highlighting characters' growth and the depth of their commitments. In the shadowy world of mafia romance, sacrifice takes on many forms—personal, professional, and moral. Characters may find themselves sacrificing their own safety, their ambitions, or their principles for the sake of love or family. These moments of sacrifice serve to underscore the intensity of the relationships at play and the profound impact of love in a world governed by power and greed.

Pursuit of Power

Power, and the relentless pursuit of it, is a central theme in mafia romance. It's not just about the physical power over others but also the internal struggle for control over one's own destiny. Characters are often depicted as being caught in the web of their organizations' power dynamics, seeking to navigate, maintain, or challenge their position within this hierarchy. The pursuit of power drives many of the conflicts in mafia romance, from territorial disputes to internal power struggles, and it often intersects with the personal growth of the characters as they seek to define what true power means to them. This theme explores the costs of power, the sacrifices made in its pursuit, and the realization that true strength often lies in vulnerability and love.

Tradition vs. Modernity

Mafia romance frequently explores the tension between tradition and modernity, reflecting the genre's roots in organized crime families that value ancient codes of honor and loyalty. Characters may find themselves at odds with the expectations imposed by their roles within these traditional structures, striving for personal autonomy or pushing against outdated norms. This theme delves into the conflict between upholding the old ways and embracing change, whether through the evolution of the mafia itself or through characters' relationships. It poses questions about the value of tradition in a modern world and the possibility of forging a new path that reconciles the past with the future.

Family Dynamics

At the heart of many mafia romance stories are the complex dynamics of family. Family in this context is not just a source of support and love but also a burden of expectations, obligations, and sometimes, manipulation. The theme of family explores the bonds that tie characters to their lineage and legacy, for better or worse. It examines the influence of family on characters' choices, the conflict between familial duty and personal desire, and the idea that family can be both a sanctuary and a prison. Through the lens of family, mafia romance narratives dissect the meaning of loyalty, the weight of heritage, and the quest for individual identity within the collective identity of the mafia family.

Struggle for Identity

Closely linked to the theme of family dynamics is the struggle for identity, a prevalent theme in mafia romance. Characters often grapple with their sense of self, torn between the roles they are born into and the people they wish to become. This struggle for identity is amplified by the clandestine nature of the mafia world, where one's true self must often be hidden behind a façade of ruthlessness and control. The genre explores how love and personal relationships become the catalyst for characters to confront and reconcile their dual identities, offering a narrative journey from self-doubt to self-acceptance. This theme resonates deeply with readers, mirroring our universal quest for authenticity in a world that often demands conformity.

Honor and Dishonor

In the mafia world, the concepts of honor and dishonor govern not just the actions but the very essence of its characters. This theme explores how characters navigate the moral compass of a world where honor might demand acts considered dishonorable by societal standards. It delves into the personal conflicts that arise when what is perceived as honorable within the mafia contradicts one's personal ethics, creating a rich ground for character development and moral dilemmas.

The Weight of Legacy

Many characters in mafia romance are born into their roles within the criminal underworld, carrying the weight of their family's legacy on their shoulders. This theme examines the burdens of expectations, the fear of failure, and the desire to forge one's own path while respecting the past. The weight of legacy challenges characters to reconcile their individual desires with their responsibilities to their heritage, offering narratives that are as much about personal growth as they are about romance.

Corruption and Redemption

Corruption, both internal and external, is a recurring theme in mafia romance, often serving as a backdrop against which the love story unfolds. Characters may struggle with their own moral corruption or fight against the corruption within their organizations or families. The theme of redemption is closely tied to this, as characters seek to cleanse themselves or their worlds of the taint of their actions or associations. This theme explores the possibility of change and the belief that love can be a redemptive force powerful enough to overcome the darkest of pasts.

The Cost of Violence

Inevitably, violence is a part of life in the mafia, and its cost is a theme that permeates many mafia romances. This theme confronts the physical, emotional, and psychological toll of living a life steeped in violence, not only on the perpetrators but also on their loved ones and victims. It questions the sustainability of such a life and the possibility of escape or change, offering a poignant commentary on the cycles of violence that characters are trapped in.

Search for Peace within Chaos

Amidst the turmoil of mafia life, the search for peace, both personal and communal, emerges as a compelling theme. Characters often yearn for a semblance of normalcy and safety—a haven within the storm of their daily existence. This theme explores the dichotomy between the chaotic world of organized crime and the human desire for peace, stability, and love. It highlights the lengths to which characters will go to protect their loved ones and carve out a space of tranquility in a life otherwise defined by danger.

Ethical Ambiguity and Moral Complexity

As characters navigate the underworld of organized crime, they often encounter situations that challenge their moral compasses, leading to ethical ambiguity and complex moral dilemmas. This theme delves into the gray areas of morality, where right and wrong are not easily distinguished, and decisions have far-reaching consequences. It explores how characters reconcile their actions with their values and how love and loyalty can complicate their sense of justice.

The Illusion of Power

While the pursuit of power is a central theme in mafia romance, an emerging narrative explores the illusion of power—how it can be both intoxicating and ultimately unsatisfying. Characters ascend to positions of authority only to find that true power lies in things that cannot be controlled, such as love, loyalty, and freedom. This theme questions the true nature of power, suggesting that vulnerability and emotional connections may offer a more authentic form of strength.

Identity and Self-Discovery

Amidst the backdrop of crime and conflict, characters often embark on journeys of self-discovery, questioning their identities and the roles they play within their families and the mafia at large. This theme focuses on the quest for personal authenticity in a world that demands conformity to rigid roles and expectations. It highlights the transformative power of love and adversity in shaping one's sense of self and the courage required to embrace one's true identity.

The Cost of Loyalty

Expanding on the theme of loyalty, modern mafia romance also examines its cost, both personally and professionally. Characters are frequently faced with decisions that test their loyalty to their families, partners, and their own principles. This theme explores the sacrifices made in the name of loyalty, questioning whether such devotion is a virtue or a chain that binds characters to a predetermined fate, and how these sacrifices impact their relationships and personal growth.

Escaping the Past

Many characters in mafia romance are haunted by their pasts—by actions they've taken, secrets they've kept, or legacies they've inherited. The theme of escaping the past examines the struggle to break free from the shadows of history to forge a new path that is not determined by previous mistakes or family expectations. It explores the idea that individuals are not defined by their pasts but by the choices they make in the present, offering narratives of hope, change, and redemption.

The Blurring of Friend and Enemy Lines

In the complex web of alliances and rivalries that characterizes the mafia world, the lines between friend and enemy are often blurred. This theme explores the fluidity of relationships within the criminal underworld, where today's ally can become tomorrow's adversary and vice versa. It delves into the strategic and personal ramifications of these shifting dynamics, highlighting the importance of trust, intuition, and the often-surprising bonds that form in the face of common goals or enemies.

Chapter 3

Popular Mafia Romance Tropes

Star-Crossed Lovers

Drawing from the timeless appeal of "Romeo and Juliet," the trope of star-crossed lovers is a staple in mafia romance. This trope explores the forbidden love between individuals from rival factions or families, embodying the genre's essence by highlighting love's power to transcend boundaries and ignite conflict. The allure of this trope lies in its exploration of the tension between societal obligations and personal desires, offering readers a narrative that champions love as an unstoppable force, even in the face of seemingly insurmountable obstacles.

Redemption Arcs

The redemption arc is a critical narrative path in mafia romance, providing characters with the opportunity to confront their past actions and seek a form of personal salvation. These arcs are compelling because they offer a journey of transformation, where characters evolve in response to love, sacrifice, or the realization of their own capacity for good. Redemption arcs not only add depth to the characters but also allow readers to engage with the story on an emotional level, rooting for characters to find peace and happiness despite their flawed natures.

The Anti-Hero

The anti-hero trope, characterized by protagonists who blur the lines between hero and villain, is particularly prominent in mafia romance. These characters often possess morally ambiguous qualities, engaging in criminal activities while also showing capacity for love, loyalty, and other redeeming traits. The appeal of the anti-hero lies in their complexity; they challenge readers' perceptions and elicit sympathy for characters who, under different circumstances, might be considered beyond redemption. This trope plays with the dichotomy of darkness and light within individuals, offering a nuanced exploration of character that enriches the narrative.

Marriage of Convenience

A trope as old as time but given a fresh twist in mafia romance is the marriage of convenience. Here, unions are often brokered for strategic alliances, to cement power, or to resolve disputes between rival families. Unlike traditional romance, where such arrangements lead straightforwardly to love, in mafia romance, these marriages are fraught with danger, secrets, and the complexities of navigating the criminal underworld. This trope delves into themes of duty versus desire, exploring how love can emerge from the most pragmatic and calculated beginnings, challenging characters to find authentic emotional connections amidst the artifice.

The Protector

The protector trope is central to many mafia romance stories, featuring a character, often the male protagonist, who takes on the role of safeguarding the heroine. This protection might stem from an obligation, a debt, or a genuine emotional connection. The dynamic creates a rich vein of narrative possibilities, exploring themes of vulnerability, trust, and the shifting power dynamics between the protector and the protected. It also allows for the development of deep emotional bonds as the protector inevitably opens up to show their more tender and caring side, breaking down the walls built by a life in the mafia.

The Innocent Caught in the Crossfire

Innocence juxtaposed with the dark, dangerous world of organized crime creates a compelling narrative contrast, and this trope explores just that. Characters who are naive or removed from the criminal world find themselves entangled in the dangerous affairs of the mafia, often through no fault of their own. This trope allows for significant character development, as the innocent are forced to adapt, survive, and sometimes even embrace the world they've been thrust into. It's a journey of discovery, resilience, and often, transformation, offering a lens through which the mafia world can be re-examined and understood anew.

The Rise to Power

A trope that resonates deeply within the genre is the rise to power, charting a character's journey from the lower ranks or from outside the mafia entirely to positions of significant influence and control. This ascent is fraught with challenges, betrayals, and moral quandaries, providing a narrative arc that is as much about personal growth as it is about gaining power. The rise to power trope examines what characters are willing to sacrifice for authority and respect and how love can either be a strength or a vulnerability in this ruthless climb to the top.

Enemies to Lovers

The "enemies to lovers" trope is a beloved narrative arc within mafia romance, setting the stage for intense emotional and often physical conflict. This dynamic pits the protagonists against each other due to familial feuds, rival factions, or personal vendettas, only for them to discover a passionate connection that transcends their initial animosity. The journey from hostility to love allows for rich character development, as individuals must confront their prejudices, loyalties, and the very foundations of their identities. This trope explores the thin line between love and hate, demonstrating how love can emerge in the most unlikely circumstances.

Secret Heir

The "secret heir" trope introduces intrigue and complexity into the mafia romance narrative, revolving around a character who is unknowingly the descendant of a powerful mafia lineage or has a child in secret with a mafia member. The revelation of this hidden legacy or offspring typically sets off a chain of events that can alter power dynamics, ignite wars, or forge new alliances. This trope delves into themes of identity, legacy, and the inherent responsibilities of belonging to a powerful family, challenging characters to navigate the dangerous waters of mafia politics and familial bonds.

Double Life

Characters leading a "double life" are a staple in mafia romance, highlighting the dichotomy between the public façade and the hidden truth of life in the mafia. This trope can apply to protagonists who are undercover agents infiltrating the mafia, or mafia members who maintain an outward appearance of legitimacy while conducting their criminal activities in secret. The tension between these two worlds offers a compelling exploration of identity, morality, and the lengths to which characters will go to protect their secrets and their hearts.

Forbidden Love

While similar to the star-crossed lovers trope, "forbidden love" in mafia romance specifically focuses on relationships that defy the strict rules and expectations of the criminal underworld. This could involve love between a mafia member and law enforcement, between rival mafia families, or even within the same organization where such relationships are taboo. The forbidden nature of the relationship amplifies the stakes, driving the narrative with the constant threat of discovery and the dire consequences that could follow. This trope plays on the allure of the prohibited, highlighting the power of love to challenge the status quo.

Revenge Plot

Revenge serves as a powerful motivator in many mafia romance stories, where characters are driven by the desire to avenge wrongs done to them or their loved ones. The pursuit of vengeance often becomes intertwined with the romantic plot, as alliances are formed, secrets are uncovered, and the line between justice and revenge blurs. This trope explores the darker aspects of the human psyche, including obsession, justice, and the possibility of forgiveness. It also raises questions about the cycle of violence and whether love can pave the way for healing and redemption.

The Gruff Exterior with a Hidden Soft Heart

A common and beloved trope within mafia romance is the character who presents a hard, unyielding exterior to the world but hides a tender, compassionate heart. This trope is often applied to male protagonists who are involved in the gritty, violent life of organized crime yet show unexpected gentleness and vulnerability to the ones they love. The contrast between their public persona and private self adds depth to their character, making their eventual emotional openness and acts of love all the more poignant and impactful.

The Bargain or Deal

In the dangerous world of the mafia, bargains and deals are the currency of survival, and they often serve as the catalyst for the central romance. A character may be forced into a relationship due to a debt, a promise, or a strategic alliance disguised as a romantic entanglement. This trope explores themes of autonomy, consent, and the unexpected paths to love, as characters navigate the terms of their arrangement and gradually uncover genuine feelings amidst the deception.

Amnesia

Amnesia provides a dramatic twist in mafia romance, where a character loses their memory of key events, relationships, or their own identity, often due to an attack or accident linked to their mafia activities. This trope allows for a unique exploration of identity and love, as characters rebuild connections without the baggage of their past, offering a fresh perspective on their relationships and allegiances. It poses questions about the nature of identity and whether love can transcend the loss of memory.

Unlikely Partnerships

The trope of unlikely partnerships, where characters from vastly different worlds or opposing sides of the law come together, highlights the genre's exploration of moral gray areas and the power of love to bridge divides. This dynamic can involve a mafia member and a cop, a criminal and a civilian, or rivals from competing factions forced to work together. The tension and eventual collaboration between such partners delve into themes of trust, redemption, and the discovery of common ground in pursuit of a shared goal or enemy.

The Bodyguard Scenario

Closely related to the protector trope, the bodyguard scenario specifically involves one character being assigned to guard another, creating a fertile ground for romantic and sexual tension. The constant physical proximity and the inherent trust involved in the bodyguard's duty to protect their charge against threats to the mafia world, both external and internal, serve to deepen the connection between the characters, often leading to forbidden or unexpected love.

Rescued from Danger

A classic but ever-compelling trope in mafia romance is the rescue scenario, where one character saves another from a perilous situation, such as a kidnapping, an assassination attempt, or a rival faction's attack. This act of saving or being saved becomes a pivotal moment in the development of the relationship, often marking the beginning of deep emotional bonds formed in the crucible of danger. It explores themes of vulnerability, gratitude, and the instinct to protect those we care about, even at great personal risk.

Chapter 4

Character Archetypes and Development

Creating compelling characters is the cornerstone of crafting an engaging mafia romance narrative. With its rich tapestry of danger, passion, and moral complexity, this genre offers a unique landscape for developing characters that resonate deeply with readers. This chapter delves into the essential character archetypes within mafia romance, highlighting the journey of character development from flawed yet redeeming protagonists to complex antagonists who challenge and enrich the narrative.

The Flawed Yet Redeeming Protagonist

In the world of mafia romance, protagonists often embody a blend of darkness and light, their characters forged in the fires of the criminal underworld yet capable of profound love, loyalty, and acts of heroism. These characters are compelling because they reflect the dual nature of humanity —our capacity for both good and evil.

Character Development: To create a protagonist who is both flawed and redeeming, it's crucial to delve into their backstory, understanding the experiences that have shaped their moral compass, fears, and desires. A well-crafted protagonist in mafia romance might grapple with the weight of their role within the mafia, struggling with the demands of loyalty to the family and their ethical boundaries. Their redemption arc often involves a journey of self-discovery spurred by love, which challenges them to confront their past actions and strive for a better future.

Relatability: Making these characters relatable involves imbuing them with vulnerabilities and desires that echo universal human experiences. Despite their involvement in organized crime, these protagonists harbor dreams, fears, and insecurities that render them human and accessible to readers.

Backstory and Inner Conflict

The foundation of a flawed yet redeeming protagonist lies in their backstory, which typically involves a history of trauma, loss, or indoctrination into the mafia lifestyle at a young age. This history shapes their worldview, influencing their actions and decisions within the narrative. It's essential to delve into the specific events that have left marks on the protagonist, whether it's the loss of a loved one to the violent world they inhabit or the burden of expectations placed upon them by their family or organization.

This backstory creates an inner conflict that the protagonist wrestles with throughout the narrative. They are torn between their loyalty to their mafia family—with its codes of honor and vengeance—and their growing awareness of the moral ambiguities and personal costs of their lifestyle. This conflict is at the core of their character development, driving their journey towards redemption.

The Journey of Redemption

The path to redemption for these protagonists is fraught with challenges and obstacles, both external and internal. It often begins with a catalyst that forces them to confront their actions and consequences. This catalyst can be the introduction of the romantic interest, whose presence and influence prompt the protagonist to question their life choices and the possibility of a different path.

As the narrative progresses, the protagonist faces situations that test their resolve, pushing them to make difficult decisions that reflect their desire to change. These moments of choice are crucial in demonstrating the character's growth, as they gradually shift from self-serving or violent actions towards those that protect, serve, or sacrifice for others, particularly for the romantic interest or innocent parties caught in the crossfire.

Vulnerability and Strength

The portrayal of vulnerability in the flawed yet redeeming protagonist is vital in making them relatable and sympathetic to readers. Their moments of doubt, fear, and emotional exposure reveal the depth of their internal struggle, humanizing them and allowing readers to connect with them on a personal level. These moments of vulnerability also provide opportunities for the character to demonstrate strength, not through physical prowess or dominance but through emotional resilience, the courage to face their past, and the determination to forge a better future.

The Role of Love and Relationships

In mafia romance, love and relationships are pivotal in the protagonist's redemption arc. The romantic interest often embodies the protagonist's aspirations for a life beyond the mafia, both as a mirror to their potential for goodness and a beacon guiding them toward change. The development of this relationship should be integral to the protagonist's transformation, with each interaction, conflict, and reconciliation pushing them closer to redemption.

The relationship challenges the protagonist to open up, trust, and ultimately prioritize someone else's well-being over their desires or safety. This shift marks a significant step in their journey, illustrating their capacity for love, sacrifice, and change.

The Complex Antagonist

Antagonists in mafia romance are not mere obstacles to the protagonists' goals but fully realized characters with motivations, complexities, and vulnerabilities. They are crucial in driving the narrative forward, presenting challenges that test the protagonists' resolve, and eliciting growth and change.

Character Development: Crafting a complex antagonist involves exploring the reasons behind their actions and their worldview. Often, they are characters who have made different choices in similar circumstances to the protagonists, acting as a mirror to what the protagonists could become if they stray from their moral path. These characters might believe in the righteousness of their cause, driven by a sense of loyalty, revenge, or a desire for power, making their confrontation with the protagonists not just a battle of strength but of ideologies.

Sympathy and Understanding: To add depth to the antagonist, consider providing glimpses into their vulnerabilities or moments of humanity. This makes them more believable and creates a more emotionally engaging narrative by blurring the lines between hero and villain, challenging readers to empathize with, if not condone, their actions.

Crafting the Complex Antagonist

Creating a complex antagonist begins with understanding their motivations. These characters often have compelling reasons for their opposition to the protagonist, rooted in personal history, a sense of betrayal, or ideological differences. Their goals are not evil for the sake of evil but are driven by desires for power, respect, protection, or revenge that they believe are justified. To craft such a character, it's crucial to develop a backstory that explains how they became the person they are, detailing the experiences that shaped their worldview and actions.

Moral Ambiguity and Relatability

One of the hallmarks of the complex antagonist is moral ambiguity. These characters operate in a world where the lines between right and wrong are often blurred, making their actions, at times, sympathetically understandable. This ambiguity forces readers to grapple with their feelings towards the antagonist, creating a tension that adds depth to the reading experience. By presenting the antagonist's perspective, their rationalizations, and the genuine emotions behind their actions, authors can foster a sense of relatability, prompting readers to question what they would do in similar circumstances.

The Antagonist's Journey

Like the protagonist, the complex antagonist undergoes a journey throughout the narrative. This journey might involve a quest for power, a desire for redemption, or a struggle with internal demons. The evolution of the antagonist, whether they find redemption, meet their downfall, or continue on their path, is a critical element of their complexity. Their interactions with the protagonist and other characters, their reactions to setbacks, and their adaptability reveal different facets of their character, making them dynamic entities within the story.

Conflict and Growth

The conflict between the protagonist and the complex antagonist is not merely physical but ideological and emotional. This conflict is the engine of the narrative, driving both characters towards growth and change. For the protagonist, the antagonist represents the darker possibilities of their world, a mirror reflecting their potential fate should they lose their moral compass. For the antagonist, the protagonist might embody the ideals or happiness they once aspired to but believe they can no longer attain. This dynamic creates a rich, emotional battleground where victories and losses are measured in more than just physical outcomes.

Sympathy and Redemption

In some narratives, the complex antagonist may be presented with their path to redemption, paralleling the protagonist's journey. This potential for change adds another layer to their complexity, suggesting that the difference between hero and villain can sometimes be a matter of choice and circumstance. Whether or not the antagonist achieves redemption, the exploration of this possibility enriches the narrative, offering a nuanced commentary on the themes of forgiveness, change, and the inherent worth of every individual.

Supporting Characters: The Backbone of the Narrative

Supporting characters play a vital role in mafia romance, providing emotional depth to the story and assisting or impeding the protagonists on their journey. These characters, from loyal lieutenants and wise advisors to family members and friends caught in the crossfire, enrich the narrative tapestry, offering alternate perspectives on the mafia world and the moral dilemmas it presents.

Character Development: Each supporting character should have a distinct voice, background, and role in the story. They can serve as confidants, sources of wisdom, comic relief, or represent the innocent lives affected by the mafia's activities. Careful development ensures that these characters contribute meaningfully to the story, influencing the protagonists' growth and the narrative's direction.

Moral Ambiguity and Relatability

One of the hallmarks of the complex antagonist is moral ambiguity. These characters operate in a world where the lines between right and wrong are often blurred, making their actions, at times, sympathetically understandable. This ambiguity forces readers to grapple with their feelings towards the antagonist, creating a tension that adds depth to the reading experience. By presenting the antagonist's perspective, their rationalizations, and the genuine emotions behind their actions, authors can foster a sense of relatability, prompting readers to question what they would do in similar circumstances.

The Antagonist's Journey

Like the protagonist, the complex antagonist undergoes a journey throughout the narrative. This journey might involve a quest for power, a desire for redemption, or a struggle with internal demons. The evolution of the antagonist, whether they find redemption, meet their downfall, or continue on their path, is a critical element of their complexity. Their interactions with the protagonist and other characters, their reactions to setbacks, and their adaptability reveal different facets of their character, making them dynamic entities within the story.

Conflict and Growth

The conflict between the protagonist and the complex antagonist is not merely physical but ideological and emotional. This conflict is the engine of the narrative, driving both characters towards growth and change. For the protagonist, the antagonist represents the darker possibilities of their world, a mirror reflecting their potential fate should they lose their moral compass. For the antagonist, the protagonist might embody the ideals or happiness they once aspired to but believe they can no longer attain. This dynamic creates a rich, emotional battleground where victories and losses are measured in more than just physical outcomes.

Sympathy and Redemption

In some narratives, the complex antagonist may be presented with their path to redemption, paralleling the protagonist's journey. This potential for change adds another layer to their complexity, suggesting that the difference between hero and villain can sometimes be a matter of choice and circumstance. Whether or not the antagonist achieves redemption, the exploration of this possibility enriches the narrative, offering a nuanced commentary on the themes of forgiveness, change, and the inherent worth of every individual.

Chapter 5

The Setting: Building the Mafia World

In the genre of mafia romance, the setting is not merely a backdrop for the narrative; it is a character in its own right, imbued with life, culture, and a palpable sense of danger. The construction of a convincing mafia world is crucial in immersing readers, providing the stage upon which the drama of love, loyalty, and betrayal unfolds. This chapter delves into the intricacies of building a rich, immersive mafia world, from the shadowy alleys of power to the luxurious halls of influence, guiding writers on how to create a setting that breathes authenticity and tension into their stories.

Understanding the Underworld

The first step in building the mafia world is to understand its foundations—its rules, hierarchy, and the codes that govern its existence. The mafia is not a monolith but a complex network of families, each with its history, traditions, and territories. Research into real-life organized crime syndicates can offer valuable insights into the structure of these families, the dynamics of power within them, and the rituals that define their members' lives.

Historical and Cultural Context: Incorporating historical and cultural details can lend authenticity to the setting. Whether your story is set in the Sicilian Mafia, the Russian Bratva, the Japanese Yakuza, or another organized crime group, understanding the specific customs, language, and values of these societies can add depth to the narrative and provide a richer backdrop for the characters' actions.

Crafting the Physical Environment

The physical environment of the mafia world plays a crucial role in setting the tone of the story. This encompasses not just the geographical location—be it the streets of New York, the countryside of Sicily, or the shores of Tokyo—but also the specific locales where the narrative unfolds. Safe houses, nightclubs, mansions, and derelict warehouses all serve as stages for key events in the story, each imbued with an atmosphere that reflects the mood of the scene.

Atmospheric Detail: Descriptive details can transform these settings from mere locations to vivid scenes that envelop the reader. The play of light in a dimly lit room, the opulence of a mafia don's office, or the starkness of a hideout can all contribute to the emotional impact of the narrative, enhancing the tension, romance, or danger of the moment.

The Social Environment

Beyond the physical, the social environment of the mafia world is defined by its networks of alliances, rivalries, and the constant undercurrent of danger that pervades interactions within and outside the organization. This is a world where trust is precious, betrayal is a constant threat, and every relationship is laden with potential peril.

Power Dynamics: Understanding and depicting the power dynamics within the mafia, between rival families, and in interactions with external entities such as law enforcement or other criminal organizations is key to building a convincing social environment. These dynamics influence every aspect of the characters' lives, from their personal relationships to their professional decisions, and must be carefully woven into the fabric of the narrative.

Incorporating Conflict

Conflict is the lifeblood of the mafia world, driving the narrative forward and shaping the characters' journeys. This can take many forms, from internal conflicts within the family to external threats from rivals or law enforcement. The setting should be constructed in a way that naturally gives rise to these conflicts, through the territories contested, the resources coveted, and the secrets hidden within the heart of the organization.

Ethical and Moral Dilemmas: The setting should also reflect the ethical and moral dilemmas inherent in the mafia world. This includes the impact of organized crime on innocent bystanders, the corruption of legal institutions, and the personal cost of living a life bound by the mafia's codes. These dilemmas can add layers of complexity to the setting, challenging characters, and readers alike to navigate the murky waters of right and wrong. We'll expound on this shortly.

Tips on crafting an authentic and immersive mafia setting

Writers must delve deep into the fabric of the organized crime world to craft an authentic and immersive mafia setting that resonates with readers and serves as a vital backdrop for the unfolding romance and drama. Here are detailed tips on achieving such a setting, ensuring that the world-building enhances the narrative and captivates the audience.

Conduct Thorough Research

Understand the Real Mafia: Start with comprehensive research into the historical and contemporary aspects of organized crime. Books, documentaries, and scholarly articles can provide insights into the operations, culture, and significant events in the history of the mafia. Pay attention to the nuances of different organizations (e.g., Sicilian Mafia, Russian Bratva, Japanese Yakuza) to portray their unique attributes accurately.

Explore Legal and Social Frameworks: Investigate the legal systems, law enforcement tactics, and societal attitudes towards organized crime in the setting of your story. This understanding can add depth to your narrative, showing not only how the mafia operates but also how it interacts with and influences the broader world.

Incorporate Cultural and Historical Context

Embed Cultural Nuances: Each mafia organization is deeply rooted in its cultural context. Incorporate elements such as language, traditions, values, and social norms into your setting. Use cultural details to enrich dialogues, ceremonies, and interpersonal interactions, lending authenticity to your characters and their world.

Utilize Historical Events: Reference real historical events or periods that have shaped the mafia's evolution. Whether your story is set in the past or present, acknowledging the impact of significant events (e.g., Prohibition Era for the American Mafia) can ground your narrative in reality.

Detail the Physical Environment

Create Vivid Locales: Describe the physical spaces where your story takes place with rich detail. From the opulent homes of mafia leaders to the gritty streets of their territories, each location should reflect the atmosphere you want to convey. Use sensory details—sights, sounds, smells—to make these settings come alive for the reader.

Use Geography to Your Advantage: Let the geography of your setting influence the plot. The isolation of a rural Sicilian estate, the bustling anonymity of Tokyo, or the stark contrasts of New York City can all impact the characters' actions and the story's dynamics.

Craft a Complex Social Structure

Define Hierarchies and Roles: Clearly outline the hierarchy within the mafia organization, from the boss down to the soldiers. Understanding each role's duties, loyalties, and codes of conduct can help you create a believable social structure that influences characters' interactions and decisions.

Show the Impact on Communities: Demonstrate how the mafia's presence affects the communities in which they operate. This might include the dual role of protectors and exploiters they play, the economic influence they wield, or the fear and respect they command among the populace.

Weave in Conflict and Tension

Highlight Internal Conflicts: The mafia world is rife with power struggles, ambition, and betrayal. Use these internal conflicts to drive the narrative, showing how alliances shift and rivalries form within the organization.

External Threats: Incorporate external pressures such as rival organizations, law enforcement pursuits, or public scrutiny. These threats can add tension and stakes to the setting, forcing characters to react and adapt.

Ethical and Moral Dilemmas

Explore the Grey Areas: Delve into the moral ambiguities of the mafia life. Present situations where characters must choose between loyalty to the mafia and their personal ethics, challenging readers to think about what they would do in similar circumstances.

Consequences of Actions: Show the repercussions of the mafia's activities, both on individuals and the community. This not only adds realism to your setting but also deepens the narrative's emotional impact.

The importance of Research and Real-World Influences

The importance of research and real-world influences in crafting an authentic and immersive mafia romance setting cannot be overstated. This foundational work is essential not only for ensuring accuracy and authenticity but also for enriching the narrative with depth and complexity. Here's a detailed exploration of why thorough research and the incorporation of real-world influences are crucial in developing a compelling mafia world.

Ensuring Authenticity

Cultural and Operational Accuracy: Understanding the inner workings of mafia organizations, their cultural roots, and how they operate in the real world is crucial for creating an authentic narrative. This includes knowledge of their hierarchical structures, codes of conduct, and the rituals that define their identity. Authenticity in these details lends credibility to the story, allowing readers to immerse themselves fully in the world you've created.

Language and Dialogue: Research helps in accurately capturing the dialects, slang, and jargon unique to the mafia milieu and its cultural context. This authenticity in dialogue enhances character development and setting, providing a more immersive reading experience. Accurate use of language also respects the cultural origins of the organization being portrayed, which is essential in today's culturally sensitive reading environment.

Enriching the Narrative

Depth and Complexity: Real-world research into the history and current activities of mafia organizations can introduce plot ideas and conflicts that add depth and complexity to the narrative. Historical events, internal power struggles, and the impact of globalization on organized crime can all serve as rich fodder for the story, allowing for a multi-layered narrative that engages readers on multiple levels.

Character Development: Understanding the real-world influences on mafia members—from the pressures of loyalty and honor to the personal toll of living a life of crime—can inform the development of complex, nuanced characters. Realistic motivations, conflicts, and growth arcs grounded in actual mafia experiences will resonate more deeply with readers, making the characters' journeys more compelling and emotionally impactful.

Enhancing Relatability and Engagement

Universal Themes: Incorporating real-world influences allows for the exploration of universal themes such as power, loyalty, betrayal, and redemption within the specific context of the mafia world. This not only enriches the narrative but also enhances its relatability, as readers can connect the story's themes to broader human experiences and moral questions.

Moral Ambiguity and Ethical Dilemmas: Research into the real-world operations and impacts of mafia organizations can highlight the moral ambiguities and ethical dilemmas inherent in their activities. Presenting these aspects in the narrative encourages readers to engage with the story on a deeper level, pondering complex moral questions and the nature of right and wrong in a world governed by its own codes.

Building a Believable World

Setting and Atmosphere: Detailed research into the locations and environments where mafia organizations operate can help in creating vivid, believable settings. From the gritty streets of urban strongholds to the secluded compounds of rural territories, understanding the real-world settings of these organizations allows writers to construct atmospheric backdrops that enhance the narrative's mood and tension.

Social Impact: Exploring the real-world influence of mafia activities on communities and societies can add a layer of realism to the narrative. This includes the economic, social, and psychological impacts on both members and non-members, providing a backdrop that reflects the complexities of life within and around organized crime.

Ethical Considerations in Portrayal

When crafting a mafia romance narrative, it's important to navigate the ethical landscape with care. While the allure of the mafia world is undeniable, it's crucial to remember that these organizations are involved in activities that have real, often harmful, impacts on individuals and communities.

Avoiding Glamorization: While the romantic and dramatic elements are central to the genre, avoiding the glamorization of criminal activities is essential. Strive to present a balanced portrayal that acknowledges the consequences and moral complexities of the mafia lifestyle.

Sensitivity to Real-world Victims: Be mindful of the real-world victims of organized crime. While your narrative is fictional, grounding your story in empathy and respect for those who have suffered due to these activities enriches the narrative's moral depth.

Incorporating Diverse Perspectives

The world of organized crime is not monolithic, and incorporating diverse perspectives within your mafia romance can add layers of complexity and authenticity to your narrative.

Multiple Viewpoints: Consider exploring the story from multiple viewpoints, including those within the mafia organization and those on its periphery—family members, law enforcement, and innocent bystanders. This approach can offer a more nuanced exploration of the narrative's themes and conflicts.

Cultural Diversity: Reflecting the global reality of organized crime, incorporating characters from various cultural backgrounds can enrich the narrative, offering diverse viewpoints and experiences. This diversity should be approached with research and sensitivity, ensuring accurate and respectful representation.

Leveraging Real-world Events

Drawing inspiration from real-world events can provide a grounded and compelling backdrop for your mafia romance narrative.

Historical and Contemporary Events: Incorporating elements inspired by actual historical events or current issues related to organized crime can lend credibility and urgency to your story. Whether it's a past mafia war, contemporary legal battles, or the impact of globalization on criminal organizations, these elements can create a resonant setting that engages readers with its realism.

Social and Political Commentary: Through the lens of your narrative, you can explore broader social and political themes, offering commentary on issues such as corruption, justice, and the socio-economic factors that foster organized crime. This approach can elevate the story, making it not only a tale of romance and intrigue but also a reflection on larger societal issues.

Authentic Dialogue and Language Use

The use of authentic dialogue and language specific to the mafia culture you're depicting can significantly enhance the immersive quality of your narrative.

Language and Dialects: Incorporating the specific dialects, slang, and terms used within the mafia culture being portrayed adds authenticity and depth to your characters' voices.

Bilingual Elements: If applicable, integrating bilingual elements or phrases native to the characters' backgrounds can add realism and texture to the dialogue, provided they are used sensitively and contextually explained for readers unfamiliar with the language.

Chapter 6

Plot Construction and Tension Building

Constructing a compelling plot and building tension are crucial elements in crafting an engaging mafia romance narrative. The intricacies of organized crime provide a rich backdrop for high stakes, moral dilemmas, and passionate romances, all of which contribute to a story that keeps readers on the edge of their seats. This chapter delves into strategies for weaving a complex plot and escalating tension that not only drives the narrative forward but also deepens the emotional and thematic resonance of the story.

Foundation of Mafia Romance Plot Construction

Establish Clear Stakes: In mafia romance, the stakes are inherently high due to the dangerous nature of organized crime. Establishing what is at risk early in the story—

whether it's the survival of the protagonist, the fate of a love interest, or the future of a mafia family—sets the groundwork for tension and conflict.

Incorporate Key Plot Points: The narrative should include pivotal plot points that propel the story forward, such as betrayals, power struggles, family secrets coming to light, and clashes with rival factions. These events serve as catalysts for character development and relationship dynamics, driving the plot toward its climax.

Interweave Romance and Crime: Balancing the romance plot with the crime plot is essential. The development of the romantic relationship should be closely tied to criminal activities and conflicts, with each aspect influencing and complicating the other. The romance can offer moments of relief and human connection amidst the tension of the mafia world.

Building Tension

Escalating Conflict: Gradually escalating the conflict within the story is key to building tension. This can involve tightening the web of danger around the protagonists, introducing new threats, or complicating existing ones. The sense that the situation is progressively worsening keeps readers invested in the outcome.

Character Internal Conflict: Tension also arises from the internal conflict experienced by the characters. Their personal struggles, moral dilemmas, and emotional turmoil add depth to the narrative and heighten the stakes. The protagonists' internal battles—torn between love, loyalty, and their own ethics—can provide a compelling undercurrent of tension.

Unpredictability and Twists: Introducing unexpected plot twists and turns keeps the narrative dynamic and unpredictable. When readers can't foresee what's coming next, their engagement and investment in the story increase. Twists can involve character betrayals, revelations of hidden agendas, or unforeseen obstacles that test the protagonists' resolve and adaptability.

Techniques for Effective Plot Construction

Foreshadowing: Employ foreshadowing to hint at future events or twists, creating a sense of anticipation and unease. This technique can be subtle, such as a seemingly offhand comment or an ominous detail in the setting, planting seeds of curiosity and foreboding in the readers' minds.

Pacing: Managing the pacing of the story is crucial in maintaining tension. Balancing faster-paced action sequences with slower, character-driven scenes ensures that the narrative maintains momentum without overwhelming the reader. Pacing can be manipulated through sentence structure, paragraph length, and chapter breaks to control the story's rhythm.

Multiple Perspectives: Utilizing multiple perspectives can enrich the plot and enhance tension. Seeing the story unfold from different characters' viewpoints—especially those on opposing sides of the conflict—offers a fuller picture of the stakes and complexities at play. This approach can also create dramatic irony, where the reader knows more than the characters, heightening anticipation.

Weaving Intricate Plots that balance Romance and Danger

Weaving intricate plots that balance romance and danger is a hallmark of compelling mafia romance narratives. This balance ensures that the story captivates readers with its emotional depth and thrilling action, maintaining engagement and investment throughout. Here are strategies to achieve this delicate equilibrium:

Intertwine Romance and Danger from the Start

Shared Stakes: Begin by establishing stakes that are inherently linked to both the romance and danger aspects of the story. For instance, the romantic interests could meet during a dangerous situation, or their relationship could directly influence the power dynamics within the mafia world. This immediate intertwining sets the stage for a narrative where love and peril are inextricably connected.

Character Connections: Ensure that the characters' backgrounds or current circumstances naturally bring romance and danger together. A romance between a mafia leader and someone from a rival faction, or between a mafia member and an undercover agent, naturally combines these elements by placing the characters in situations where their loyalties are tested.

Develop Multi-layered Characters

Conflicting Desires: Craft characters with conflicting desires and duties that place them at the crossroads of romance and danger. A protagonist might struggle between their growing love for someone and their loyalty to their mafia family, creating internal conflict that drives the narrative forward.

Complex Antagonists: Utilize antagonists who have personal stakes in both the romantic and dangerous aspects of the plot. An antagonist with a vendetta against the protagonist's love interest, for example, can heighten tension in both domains simultaneously.

Use Subplots to Enrich the Main Narrative

Parallel Subplots: Incorporate subplots that mirror or contrast the main plot, using them to explore different facets of romance and danger. A subplot involving a secondary character's romantic entanglement can provide insights into the risks and rewards of love in a dangerous world, enriching the overall narrative.

Interconnected Subplots: Ensure subplots are interconnected with the main storyline in ways that escalate the central conflict and tension. For example, a subplot involving a betrayal within the mafia could jeopardize both the safety and relationship of the main characters, linking back to the primary narrative thread.

Manipulate Pacing to Enhance Tension

Alternating Pacing: Alternate between fast-paced, action-driven scenes and slower, emotionally charged romantic scenes. This variation in pacing keeps readers engaged, providing breathers while continuously building tension towards the climax.

Climactic Convergence: Design the plot so that the climax resolves both the romantic and danger arcs simultaneously. This convergence can provide a satisfying resolution that ties up loose ends and reinforces the connection between love and peril in the narrative.

Employ Themes as Connecting Threads

Shared Themes: Utilize recurring themes that bridge romance and danger. Themes like loyalty, sacrifice, and redemption can be explored through both the romantic relationship and the criminal activities, serving as a thematic undercurrent that ties the narrative together.

Moral Dilemmas: Present characters with moral dilemmas that test their values in both romantic and dangerous situations. How they navigate these dilemmas can drive the plot and deepen the thematic resonance of the story.

Leverage Setting and Atmosphere

Atmospheric Tension: Use the setting to create an atmosphere that enhances both the romantic and dangerous elements of the story. A secluded safe house, for example, can be the perfect setting for both intimate moments and tense standoffs.

Symbolic Locations: Choose locations that symbolize the intersection of romance and danger. The ruins of a once-grand estate might reflect the perilous decay of the mafia world while serving as a backdrop for a burgeoning romance, adding layers of meaning to the narrative.

Building Suspense and Maintaining Reader Engagement

Building suspense and maintaining reader engagement are crucial techniques in crafting a captivating mafia romance story. These techniques not only keep the pages turning but also deepen the emotional investment of the reader. Here are strategies to weave suspense into the fabric of your narrative and ensure your audience remains hooked from start to finish.

Establish High Stakes Early On

Personal and Universal Stakes: Clearly outline what's at risk, both on a personal level for the characters and within the broader context of the mafia world. High stakes create a sense of urgency and consequence, laying the foundation for suspense.

Immediate Threats: Introduce a sense of danger or an immediate threat early in the story. This could be a rival mafia family making moves on the protagonist's territory or a personal vendetta that puts the love interest in danger.

Use Cliffhangers and Unanswered Questions

Chapter Endings: Employ cliffhangers at the end of chapters to create compelling reasons for readers to keep going.

This could be an unexpected revelation, a character in peril, or a dramatic confrontation.

Strategic Information Withholding: Withhold crucial information for as long as possible, revealing it at key moments to maximize impact. Keeping readers guessing about characters' true motivations or the outcome of certain events builds suspense.

Implement Multiple Perspectives

Insider and Outsider Views: Utilize multiple points of view to offer readers insight into the complex dynamics of the mafia world from both inside and outside. This can create tension as readers are privy to information that some characters might not know.

Contrasting Perspectives: Showing events from contrasting perspectives can heighten suspense by revealing the stakes involved for all parties. This technique also enriches character development and plot complexity.

Create a Ticking Clock Scenario

Deadline-Driven Plot: Introduce a 'ticking clock' element where characters must achieve their goals within a set time-frame, adding urgency to their actions and decisions.

Countdown Elements: Use countdowns or deadlines tied to significant events, such as a rival gang's move, a court trial, or an impending attack, to heighten suspense and drive the narrative forward.

Incorporate Twists and Turns

Unexpected Revelations: Craft plot twists that challenge the reader's and characters' expectations. Twists that upend the status quo or reveal hidden alliances and betrayals keep the story unpredictable.

Layered Secrets: Develop characters with secrets that are gradually unveiled, adding depth to their motivations and past actions. The revelation of these secrets can alter the course of relationships and the plot.

Leverage Internal Conflict

Emotional Dilemmas: Highlight the internal conflicts and emotional dilemmas faced by characters, particularly those that pit personal desires against duties to the mafia. These conflicts add psychological suspense and deepen reader engagement.

Moral Ambiguity: Explore the moral ambiguity inherent in the mafia lifestyle, forcing characters to make difficult choices. This not only builds suspense but also invites readers to ponder what they would do in similar situations.

Use Descriptive Language to Build Atmosphere

Sensory Details: Employ rich, sensory details to create an atmosphere that reflects the mood of the narrative. The way you describe a setting can amplify suspense, whether it's the ominous quiet of a deserted street or the tense atmosphere of a mafia meeting.

Symbolism and Foreshadowing: Use symbolic elements and foreshadowing to hint at future events or the true nature of characters. This technique creates a layer of suspense as readers try to piece together clues.

Conclusion

Building suspense and maintaining reader engagement in mafia romance requires a careful balance of plot pacing, character development, and strategic use of narrative techniques. By establishing high stakes, utilizing cliffhangers, incorporating multiple perspectives, creating a ticking clock scenario, and employing twists and turns, you can craft stories that keep readers riveted. Additionally, leveraging internal conflict and using descriptive language to build atmosphere can deepen the emotional resonance of the story, making the suspense all the more compelling. Through these techniques, your mafia romance novel can achieve a gripping narrative that captivates and entertains from beginning to end.

Chapter 7

Crafting Steamy Scenes with Depth in Mafia Romances

In the world of mafia romance, the allure goes beyond the thrill of danger and power struggles—it ventures into the realm of passion, where steamy scenes between characters are not just physical encounters but emotional voyages that reveal depth, vulnerability, and the complex interplay of dominance and desire. Writing steamy scenes that resonate with readers requires a nuanced approach, blending the raw intensity of attraction with the emotional and psychological layers that define the characters involved. This chapter aims to guide authors through the process of crafting such scenes, ensuring they contribute to the narrative's emotional depth and character development while also satisfying the readers' craving for passion and intimacy.

Understanding the Dynamics

The Power Play

Mafia romances inherently involve power dynamics that can add a tantalizing edge to romantic encounters. The key is to navigate these dynamics with sensitivity, ensuring that the power play enhances the consensual and mutual exploration of desires. Characters might wield power in the outside world, but in the realm of intimacy, vulnerability and equality become the cornerstone of a meaningful connection.

Emotional Stakes

Steamy scenes must carry emotional weight. Each encounter should reveal something new about the characters, whether it's an unguarded moment of vulnerability, a revelation of deep-seated fears, or an expression of unconditional acceptance. The emotional stakes are heightened in a mafia romance, where love and passion often bloom in the shadow of danger and betrayal.

Setting the Scene

Integrating the Mafia Context

The mafia backdrop provides a rich tapestry against which steamy scenes unfold. Use the tension and danger inherent in the mafia world to fuel the urgency and intensity of the characters' encounters. Whether it's a stolen moment amidst chaos or a passionate reunion after a perilous mission, the context should amplify the scene's emotional impact.

Sensory Details

Create an immersive experience by invoking the five senses. The scent of rain on cobblestone streets after a secret meeting, the feel of silk sheets in a hidden safe house, or the sound of distant sirens blending with whispered declarations of love can all serve to deepen the scene's atmosphere and emotional resonance.

Building Emotional Depth

Revealing Inner Worlds

Use steamy scenes as windows into the characters' inner worlds. Through their most intimate moments, reveal their fears, desires, and conflicts. Show how the power dynamics of their external world influence their personal vulnerabilities and strengths in love and intimacy.

The Dance of Dominance and Vulnerability

In mafia romances, characters often wear masks of strength and dominance. In steamy scenes, allow these masks to slip, revealing the vulnerability and longing beneath. This dance between strength and vulnerability adds layers to the romance, making each encounter a journey of emotional discovery.

Dialogue and Inner Monologue

Authentic Dialogue

Dialogue during steamy scenes should feel authentic and in the moment, reflecting the characters' personalities and emotional states. It can range from tender whispers to raw, unguarded expressions of desire, serving as a powerful tool for character development and emotional depth.

Inner Monologue

Inner monologues offer insight into the characters' thoughts and feelings, adding layers to the physical connection. Use these moments to explore the characters' reflections on their relationship, the risks they're taking, and the depth of their feelings, enhancing the scene's emotional impact.

Consent and Agency

Navigating Consent

In mafia romances, where power and control are central themes, navigating consent is crucial. Ensure that steamy scenes are grounded in mutual desire and respect, allowing both characters to express their agency and boundaries. This not only enriches the narrative but also fosters a healthy model of intimacy.

Empowering Characters

Empower your characters to explore their desires and boundaries within the safety of their relationship. This empowerment is especially significant for characters who may wield less power in the outside world, providing a space where they feel seen, valued, and respected.

Aftermath and Consequences

Emotional Aftermath

Steamy scenes should have consequences for the characters' emotional journey. Whether it's a deepening of trust, the surfacing of new insecurities, or a shift in the relationship dynamics, the aftermath of these encounters should propel the narrative forward.

Integrating Plot Progression

Use the aftermath of steamy scenes to advance the plot. Perhaps a character reveals a crucial piece of information in a moment of vulnerability, or the encounter leads to a decision that alters their path. The key is to ensure that these scenes are integral to the story's development, not just isolated moments of passion.

Understanding the Role of Steamy Scenes

Emotional Connection: Beyond their immediate allure, steamy scenes are powerful tools for exploring the emotional connection between characters. They can reveal vulnerabilities, deepen bonds, and serve as a catalyst for character growth and relationship dynamics.

Advancing the Plot: Each steamy scene should serve a purpose beyond mere titillation. Whether it's marking a turning point in the relationship, revealing hidden truths, or setting the stage for future conflict, the scene should contribute to advancing the plot or deepening the narrative.

Crafting Tasteful yet Passionate Scenes

Focus on Sensory Details: To create a scene that's both tasteful and passionate, emphasize the sensory experiences of the characters—touch, taste, smell, sight, and sound. This approach allows readers to immerse themselves in the moment, experiencing the characters' emotions and connections deeply.

Build Anticipation: The lead-up to a steamy scene is as important as the scene itself. Building anticipation through flirtation, tension, and emotional stakes can make the eventual culmination more impactful and satisfying. This buildup also provides a natural pace to the narrative, ensuring that the scene feels earned.

Balancing Explicit Content with Emotional Depth

Know Your Audience: The level of explicitness in your steamy scenes should be tailored to your audience's expectations and the overall tone of your book. It's possible to convey passion and intensity without explicit detail if that suits your story and readership better.

Emotional Resonance: Balance physical descriptions with the emotional and psychological experience of the characters. The thoughts, feelings, and desires that accompany the physical acts can provide a deeper understanding of the characters and their relationship, elevating the scene beyond the physical to the profoundly emotional.

Consent and Communication: Portraying consent and communication between characters not only ensures that the scenes are respectful but also adds to their depth and realism. Moments of consent can be woven into the narrative seamlessly, enhancing the connection and trust between characters.

Integrating Steamy Scenes into the Mafia Context

Reflecting the Stakes: The stakes are inherently high in a mafia romance story, and this tension should permeate steamy scenes as well. The danger and intensity of the mafia world can heighten the passion and urgency of these moments, reflecting the characters' awareness of the risks they face.

Using Conflict: The inherent conflicts of the mafia lifestyle —loyalties, secrets, and dangers—can add layers to steamy scenes. These elements can create a backdrop of emotional complexity, making the moments of intimacy more poignant and meaningful.

Chapter 8

The Power of Plot Twists in Storytelling

In the captivating world of mafia romance, the ability to surprise readers with well-crafted plot twists and maintain their engagement throughout the narrative is essential. A compelling twist not only reinvigorates the storyline but also deepens the reader's investment in the characters and their fates. This chapter explores strategies for incorporating twists effectively and techniques to keep readers hooked from beginning to end.

The Essence of a Plot Twist

A plot twist is a sudden, unexpected change in the direction of a narrative designed to surprise readers and challenge their assumptions about the story's trajectory. The most impactful plot twists are those that are both surprising and inevitable, in hindsight—a delicate balance that requires careful planning and execution.

Mafia romance novels, by their nature, weave together the tender vulnerabilities of love with the harsh realities of a life shadowed by crime and power struggles. Plot twists in this context are not merely narrative devices but essential elements that drive the story forward, revealing the depths of characters, the intensity of their loyalties, and the price of their desires.

Types of Plot Twists

• **Revelatory Twists:** Unveil hidden truths about characters, settings, or events that cast the narrative in a new light.

• **Perceptual Twists:** Shift the reader's understanding or perspective of the story, often by revealing new information that changes the context of previous events.

• **Situational Twists:** Alter the storyline's direction through unexpected events or decisions that defy the anticipated outcome.

Crafting Effective Plot Twists

Foundation and Foreshadowing

Effective plot twists are built on a foundation of subtle clues and foreshadowing. The twist should emerge naturally from the narrative, rooted in the characters' actions and the story's logic. Foreshadowing involves planting seeds early in the story that, upon reflection, make the twist seem inevitable.

Surprise and Inevitability

The power of a plot twist lies in its ability to surprise readers while also feeling inevitable in retrospect. This balance is achieved by ensuring the twist is not arbitrary but is deeply interconnected with the story's themes, character arcs, and narrative structure.

Emotional Impact

Plot twists should have a significant emotional impact, deepening readers' investment in the characters and the story. Whether it's a betrayal, a revelation of identity, or a shift in allegiance, the twist should challenge the characters' and readers' emotional understanding of the narrative.

Psychological Impact on Readers

Engagement and Investment

Plot twists engage readers by disrupting their expectations and inviting them to re-evaluate the story. This active engagement fosters a deeper emotional investment in the narrative and its characters as readers eagerly anticipate how the twist will affect the story's outcome.

Cognitive Dissonance and Resolution

A well-crafted plot twist induces cognitive dissonance, challenging readers' understanding of the narrative. The resolution of this dissonance, as readers integrate the new information into their understanding of the story, enhances their satisfaction and emotional response to the narrative.

Understanding the Power of Plot Twists

Revealing Hidden Motives: A well-placed twist can unveil hidden motives, altering the reader's understanding of a character's actions. For example, a seemingly loyal consigliere revealed to be orchestrating a coup can turn the narrative on its head, challenging both characters and readers to reassess their assumptions.

Altering Relationship Dynamics: Twists can dramatically shift relationship dynamics, providing depth and complexity. A revelation that the protagonist's love interest has been keeping secrets related to their mafia family can test the strength of their bond, pushing the narrative into new emotional territory.

Crafting Effective Plot Twists

Foreshadowing: Subtle hints and foreshadowing can prime readers for a twist without giving it away, creating a sense of anticipation. Clues can be woven into the narrative through dialogue, character behavior, or seemingly inconsequential events, building up to the twist in a way that feels both surprising and inevitable.

Timing: The impact of a plot twist relies heavily on its timing. Placing a twist at a narrative crossroads—such as the climax of a subplot or just when the main conflict appears to be resolving—can maximize its effect, propelling the story into its next phase with renewed momentum.

Lay the Groundwork with Subtlety

Plant Seeds Early: Introduce subtle clues or foreshadowing elements early in the narrative that hint at the twist without revealing it outright. These could be overlooked details, ambiguous conversations, or characters' seemingly minor actions that gain significance in hindsight.

Use Misdirection: Employ misdirection to lead readers (and often characters) to believe in a different outcome. This can involve highlighting a red herring or focusing attention away from the actual twist. The key is to make the misdirection believable without making the eventual twist feel unearned or deceptive.

Develop Deeply Flawed Characters

Complex Motivations: Create characters with complex motivations that justify a wide range of actions, including potential betrayals. This depth ensures that when a character does betray the protagonist or reveals a shocking secret, it aligns with their established personality and backstory, even if it's unexpected.

Dynamic Relationships: Foster dynamic relationships between characters that contain the potential for both loyalty and betrayal. Tension within these relationships can stem from past conflicts, differing goals, or secret affiliations, making any resulting twists feel integral to the character dynamics.

Master the Art of Timing

Strategic Placement: Position your plot twists at pivotal moments in the story, such as the climax of a subplot, the end of an act, or right before a significant turning point. The timing can amplify the impact of the twist, reshaping the narrative's direction and reinvigorating the reader's engagement.

Pace Your Revelations: Space out multiple twists or revelations to maintain a steady build-up of suspense and surprise throughout the story. This pacing ensures that the narrative maintains momentum and keeps readers guessing.

Ensure Twists Serve the Narrative

Advance the Plot or Character Development: Every twist should serve to advance the plot or deepen character development. Whether it's revealing a character's true allegiance, uncovering a hidden enemy, or exposing a secret past, the twist should have lasting consequences that propel the story forward.

Enhance Emotional Depth: Use twists to explore new emotional depths in your characters. A betrayal can test the protagonist's resilience, reveal their vulnerabilities, or force them to confront their fears, facilitating growth and change.

Craft Believable Betrayals

Motivated Actions: Ensure that betrayals are motivated by believable reasons that stem from the character's experiences, desires, or fears. A well-motivated betrayal, even if surprising, should feel inevitable in retrospect, rooted in the character's established traits and narrative context.

Foreshadowed Consequences: Foreshadow the consequences of potential betrayals throughout the story, hinting at the stakes involved. This not only builds tension but also prepares readers for the emotional and narrative fallout, making the eventual revelation more impactful.

Utilize Reader Expectations

Play with Tropes: Take advantage of genre tropes and reader expectations by subverting or twisting them in unexpected ways. For example, if the genre typically features a betrayal by a close confidant, consider a twist where the apparent traitor actually remains loyal, revealing an unexpected enemy instead.

Build Suspense with Uncertainty: Keep readers on edge by cultivating an atmosphere of uncertainty. When readers are unsure of whom to trust or what to believe, the impact of a well-executed twist or betrayal is significantly heightened.

Keeping Readers Hooked

Emotional Stakes: Elevating the emotional stakes of the story ensures that readers remain invested in the characters' journeys. This can involve personal dilemmas, sacrifices, or moments of vulnerability that resonate with readers on a deep level, making them eager to see how these challenges will be overcome.

Pacing Variations: Varying the pacing of the narrative can keep readers engaged, alternating between intense action sequences and quieter, character-driven moments. This dynamic pacing prevents predictability, maintaining suspense and intrigue throughout the story.

Character Depth: Developing multi-dimensional characters whose fates readers care about is crucial for maintaining engagement. Characters with complex motivations, flaws, and growth arcs can make readers invested in their development, eager to follow them through twists and turns.

Avoiding Overuse

While plot twists are powerful tools, their impact can be diluted by overuse. Striking the right balance ensures that each twist has maximum impact, contributing to the story's emotional depth and narrative momentum without overwhelming the reader or detracting from the romance at the heart of the novel.

Examples of Incorporating Twists

Betrayal Within the Ranks: A trusted member of the protagonist's inner circle revealed as a traitor can shake the foundations of the mafia family, introducing new conflicts and alliances that keep the narrative dynamic.

Unexpected Alliances: Forming alliances with unlikely characters or rival factions can offer fresh narrative paths, challenging characters to navigate unfamiliar territory and readers to question their perceptions.

Hidden Past: Uncovering a character's hidden past or secret identity can redefine their role within the story, offering new insights into their actions and motivations.

Chapter 9

How to Create Satisfying Redemption Arcs

Creating satisfying redemption arcs in mafia romance involves a delicate balance of character development, moral complexity, and narrative pacing. These arcs not only offer characters a path to atonement but also deepen the emotional resonance of the story, making the journey toward redemption both compelling and believable. Here's how to craft redemption arcs that engage and satisfy readers:

Establish a Clear Need for Redemption

Acknowledge Past Wrongs: Start by clearly establishing the reasons why a character needs redemption. This could involve past crimes, moral failings, or specific actions that have caused harm to others. The character's need for redemption should be recognized by both the character themselves and the reader, creating a foundation for their journey.

Show the Impact: Demonstrate the impact of the character's actions on themselves and those around them. This not only highlights the stakes involved in their redemption but also sets up the emotional payoff when they begin to make amends.

Develop a Genuine Desire to Change

Motivation: The character must have a compelling, genuine reason to seek redemption. This motivation can be sparked by love, the realization of their wrongdoings, or a desire for a different life. Whatever the reason, it should drive the character's actions and decisions throughout their arc.

Challenges: Redemption is not an easy path. Present your character with challenges that test their commitment to change, such as facing the consequences of their past actions, making difficult choices that go against their previous nature, or overcoming external skepticism and resistance.

Show Incremental Progress and Setbacks

Small Victories: Show the character making incremental progress on their path to redemption. This could be through acts of kindness, making amends to those they've wronged, or standing up for what's right, even when it's difficult. These moments should build on one another, illustrating the character's growth over time.

Realistic Setbacks: Characters seeking redemption will inevitably face setbacks. These moments are crucial for adding depth and realism to the arc. How the character responds to setbacks, whether they revert to old habits or find new strength to persevere, can significantly impact the arc's authenticity and emotional impact.

Integrate the Redemption Arc with the Romance

Interconnected Growth: The redemption arc should be deeply intertwined with the development of the romantic relationship. The love interest can serve as a catalyst for change, offering support, challenge, or a reason to strive for a better self. However, the character's desire to change should ultimately be self-motivated, ensuring their growth is personal and not solely for the sake of romance.

Mutual Healing: Incorporate elements of mutual healing and growth, where both characters, not just the one seeking redemption, learn and change through their relationship. This dynamic emphasizes that redemption is not a solitary journey but one that can be bolstered by love and connection.

Culminate in a Moment of Reckoning

Confrontation with the Past: A pivotal moment in any redemption arc is the confrontation with the past. This can be a literal confrontation with people from the character's past, a situation that mirrors past mistakes, or an internal reckoning where the character fully acknowledges their wrongdoings and their impact.

Act of Sacrifice: Often, redemption arcs culminate in an act of sacrifice, where the character must give up something significant for the greater good or to protect others. This act should be a testament to their change, demonstrating their commitment to a new path.

Provide a Resolution that Feels Earned

Not Without Consequences: Redemption does not erase the past. Ensure that the character's redemption feels earned, with tangible consequences for their actions still evident. This can lend a sense of realism and gravity to their journey.

New Identity: By the arc's conclusion, the character should have forged a new identity for themselves, one that acknowledges their past but also looks forward to the future. This identity should reflect their growth, the lessons they've learned, and their aspirations moving forward.

* * *

Crafting satisfying redemption arcs requires a nuanced understanding of character motivation, the capacity for change, and the power of love and support in facilitating transformation. By focusing on genuine growth, realistic challenges, and emotional depth, writers can create redemption arcs that not only captivate readers but also offer a profound exploration of the human capacity for change and atonement.

Chapter 10

Nearing Publication

Writing your first mafia romance book is an exhilarating journey that takes you deep into the heart of passion, danger, and loyalty. This chapter guides you through the initial steps of conceptualizing your story to the thrilling moment of publication, offering insights and strategies to navigate the complex landscape of writing and publishing a mafia romance novel.

Conceptualization and Planning

Finding Your Unique Angle

Mafia romance, with its blend of danger, passion, and complex moral dilemmas, offers a rich canvas for story-telling. Begin by defining your unique angle—consider what aspects of the mafia world intrigue you and how you can weave these elements into a compelling romance. Research the genre to understand its conventions and reader expectations, but don't be afraid to introduce fresh perspectives and themes.

Building Your World

The mafia world is steeped in its own codes, traditions, and hierarchies. Creating a believable, immersive world requires thorough research into the workings of organized crime, from its familial structures to its business operations. This backdrop will not only enrich your narrative but also provide a solid foundation for your characters' actions and motivations.

Character Development

In mafia romance, characters must navigate the treacherous waters of love and loyalty within a dangerous world. Develop multidimensional characters whose emotional journeys are intertwined with the mafia setting. Consider how the mafia's values and conflicts will shape their desires, fears, and relationships, making them compelling to readers.

Drafting Your Novel

Drafting, revising, and publishing a mafia romance novel is a journey filled with challenges and triumphs. This chapter delves into the step-by-step process of bringing your mafia romance story from an initial idea to a published book, highlighting the importance of each stage in the process.

Outlining Your Narrative

Begin with a detailed outline that maps out the key events of your story, including the development of the romance, the central conflict, and the resolution. Consider how the mafia setting influences the plot and characters, weaving in elements of tension, loyalty, and danger.

Writing the First Draft

Focus on getting your story onto the page, embracing the creative flow without worrying about mistakes or inconsistencies. Allow yourself to explore different directions and deepen your understanding of your characters and their world.

Revising Your Manuscript

The First Pass: Structural Edits

After completing your first draft, take a step back before returning to your manuscript with fresh eyes. Evaluate the structure of your story, looking for plot holes, pacing issues, and opportunities to enhance the emotional and thematic depth of your narrative.

Subsequent Revisions: Refining Your Story

Engage in multiple rounds of revisions, focusing on different aspects of your manuscript each time—character development, dialogue, setting details, and scene effectiveness. This iterative process helps refine your story into a polished, cohesive novel.

The Editing Journey

Types of Editing

Understand the different types of editing—developmental, line, and copy editing—and how each can improve your manuscript. Developmental editing focuses on big-picture elements like plot and character arcs, while line and copy editing refine your prose and corrects grammatical errors.

Professional Editing

Invest in a professional editor with experience in the mafia romance genre. An editor can provide invaluable feedback on your manuscript's strengths and weaknesses, offering suggestions for improvement that you might not see on your own.

Feedback and editing are critical components of preparing your mafia romance novel for the world while choosing the right publishing path sets the stage for your book's journey to readers. This chapter explores these crucial steps in detail, offering guidance to ensure your novel reaches its full potential.

The Role of Feedback in the Writing Process

Beta Readers and Critique Partners

Engage with beta readers and critique partners who can provide constructive feedback on your manuscript. Choose individuals who are familiar with the mafia romance genre and your target audience to ensure relevant and useful insights.

Processing and Implementing Feedback

Evaluate the feedback critically, identifying common themes or issues raised by your readers. Prioritize changes that align with your vision for the story, and be willing to revise deeply to enhance your novel's impact.

Choosing the Right Publishing Path

Evaluating Your Goals and Preferences

Reflect on your goals as an author and your preferences for the publishing process. Do you seek the validation and support of traditional publishing, or do you prefer the autonomy and flexibility of self-publishing?

Navigating Traditional Publishing

If you choose traditional publishing, research agents and publishers who specialize in mafia romance. Tailor your query letters to each recipient, highlighting what makes your novel stand out in the genre.

Embracing Self-Publishing

For self-publishing authors, focus on producing a high-quality book by investing in professional editing, cover design, and formatting. Explore various platforms for publishing and distributing your novel, and develop a robust marketing strategy to reach your audience.

Chapter 11

The Big "M"

In the fiercely competitive landscape of romance publishing, effectively marketing and promoting your mafia romance novel is crucial to standing out and capturing the interest of readers. Mafia romances, with their unique blend of danger, passion, and loyalty, offer ample opportunities for creative marketing strategies that can entice readers who crave stories where love battles against the backdrop of the criminal underworld. This chapter provides a comprehensive guide to marketing and promoting mafia romances, from building an engaging author brand to leveraging digital platforms and creating buzz around your book.

Building an Engaging Author Brand

Establishing Your Online Presence

Create a professional and engaging online presence across various platforms, such as a dedicated author website, social media profiles, and author pages on Amazon and Goodreads. Your online presence should reflect the themes and aesthetic of your mafia romance novels, creating a cohesive brand that appeals to your target audience.

Engaging with Your Audience

Regularly interact with your audience through social media, email newsletters, and author events. Share behind-the-scenes glimpses of your writing process, insights into your characters and world, and teasers of upcoming projects. Building a relationship with your readers can turn casual readers into loyal fans.

Utilizing Social Media Effectively

Choosing the Right Platforms

Identify the social media platforms where your target audience is most active, whether it's Instagram, Twitter, Facebook, or TikTok. Focus your efforts on these platforms to maximize engagement and reach.

Creating Shareable Content

Produce content that is not only relevant to your mafia romance novels but is also engaging and shareable. This can include aesthetically pleasing book quotes, character art, interactive polls about plot twists or character decisions, and short video teasers.

Leveraging Reader Communities

Goodreads and Book Clubs

Goodreads is a valuable platform for connecting with avid readers. Create an author profile, list your books, and engage with reader communities interested in mafia romances. Consider reaching out to book clubs that focus on romance or specifically mafia romance, offering your book for their next read and proposing a Q&A session with the author.

Online Book Tours and Blog Features

Organize online book tours by collaborating with bloggers and influencers in the romance genre. Provide them with review copies, exclusive interviews, and guest posts to generate buzz around your novel. Blog features and reviews can significantly enhance visibility and credibility among potential readers.

Advanced Reader Copies (ARCs) and Reviews

Distributing ARCs

Advance Reader Copies (ARCs) are a powerful tool for generating early buzz and garnering reviews before your book's official release. Distribute ARCs to book bloggers, reviewers, and readers who are influencers within the mafia romance community.

Encouraging Reviews

Reviews are crucial for building trust and credibility with potential readers. Encourage readers to leave honest reviews on platforms like Amazon, Goodreads, and social media. Positive word-of-mouth and reviews can significantly impact your book's visibility and sales.

Promotional Strategies and Advertising

Discount Promotions and Giveaways

Running discount promotions or organizing giveaways for your mafia romance novel can attract new readers and generate buzz. Utilize platforms like BookBub or your own social media channels to announce these promotions.

Paid Advertising

Consider investing in paid advertising through platforms such as Amazon Ads, Facebook Ads, or BookBub. Target your ads to reach readers interested in the romance genre, specifically those who have shown an interest in mafia or dark romance novels.

Networking and Collaborations

Collaborating with Other Authors

Network with other authors in the mafia romance genre for cross-promotion opportunities. Collaborations can include joint giveaways, anthology projects, or social media takeovers, helping you reach a wider audience.

Participating in Genre-Specific Events

Attend romance or crime fiction writing conferences, book fairs, and virtual events. Participating in panels, signings, and author meet-and-greets can increase your visibility and allow you to connect directly with fans of the genre.

Crafting an Immersive Launch Experience

Virtual Launch Events

With the rise of digital platforms, virtual launch events have become a powerful tool for authors. Host a live reading of your mafia romance novel on platforms like Instagram Live, Facebook Live, or Zoom. Incorporate interactive elements such as Q&A sessions, discussions about the inspiration behind your book, and virtual meet-and-greets. This not only promotes your book but also strengthens your connection with your audience.

Collaborative Launches

Consider collaborating with other authors who are releasing mafia romance novels around the same time. Joint launches can attract wider attention, pooling audiences and increasing visibility for all involved. This could involve shared online events, bundle giveaways, or collective social media campaigns.

Utilizing Multimedia Content

Book Trailers

Create a compelling book trailer that captures the essence of your mafia romance novel. Book trailers can be a dynamic way to engage potential readers, offering a visual and auditory glimpse into the story's mood and themes. Share your trailer on social media, your website, and YouTube to reach a broader audience.

Podcasts and Interviews

Appear on podcasts that cater to romance readers or focus on the writing process. Interviews can provide an in-depth look at your journey, the inspirations behind your mafia romance novel, and what readers can expect from your story. This format allows for a more personal connection with potential readers.

Enhancing Reader Engagement Post-Launch

Reader Challenges and Contests

Engage your audience with creative challenges and contests post-launch. For instance, invite readers to create fan art or playlists inspired by your book or write their own short scene featuring your characters. Offer prizes that tie back to your book, such as signed copies, exclusive merchandise, or the chance to name a character in your next novel.

Serialized Content and Bonus Material

Keep readers engaged by releasing serialized content or bonus material related to your mafia romance novel. This could include short stories or novellas that delve into the backstory of secondary characters, alternate POVs on pivotal scenes, or teasers of upcoming books. Serialized content can maintain reader interest and build anticipation for future works.

Strategic Use of Analytics and Feedback

Analytics and Ad Optimization

For authors investing in paid advertising, closely monitor the performance of your ads across different platforms. Use analytics to understand which ads are most effective in reaching your target audience and adjust your strategies accordingly. This ensures that your marketing budget is being used efficiently to maximize book visibility.

Gathering and Acting on Reader Feedback

Collect feedback from readers through reviews, social media interactions, and direct communication. Understanding what readers loved about your mafia romance novel—or what they felt was missing—can provide invaluable insights for future projects. Act on this feedback to refine your writing and marketing strategies, ensuring that your next book resonates even more strongly with your audience.

Continuous Learning and Adaptation

Stay Informed About Market Trends

The romance genre, including its mafia romance subgenre, is ever-evolving. Stay informed about market trends, reader preferences, and emerging platforms for book promotion. Being adaptable and willing to try new marketing tactics can help you stay relevant and continue to captivate your audience.

Professional Development

Invest in your professional development as an author and marketer. Attend workshops, webinars, and conferences focused on writing, publishing, and book marketing.

Networking with industry professionals and other authors can provide new opportunities for collaboration and promotion, as well as fresh insights into effective marketing strategies.

Conclusion

Marketing and promoting a mafia romance novel is an ongoing process that extends beyond the book's launch. It involves building and maintaining a strong connection with your audience, continuously adapting to market trends, and exploring innovative ways to engage readers. By employing a mix of traditional and digital marketing strategies, creating immersive and interactive content, and leveraging feedback and analytics, authors can effectively promote their mafia romance novels and build a loyal readership eager for their next enthralling tale.

Chapter 12

Studying the Successful Ones

To hone the craft of writing mafia romance, studying the works of successful authors in the genre is invaluable. Below are notable books and mafia romance authors who have made significant contributions to the mafia romance landscape. They offer a range of approaches to storytelling, character development, and world-building that can serve as both inspiration and instruction.

Mafia Romance Authors and Their Notable Works

• **Sarah Brianne** - Known for her "Made Men" series, Brianne dives deep into the lives of those entangled with the mafia. *Nero* and *Vincent* are standout entries, offering readers a blend of intense romance and the complexities of mafia loyalty.

• **Corinne Michaels** - Her "Salvation Series" showcases the intertwining of military and mafia elements, providing a unique take on the genre. *Consolation* and *Conviction* explore themes of loss, love, and redemption.

• **Bethany-Kris** - A prolific author in the genre, her "Filthy Marcellos" series is highly regarded for its detailed world-building and character depth. *Lucian* introduces readers to a compelling mafia world filled with danger and desire.

• **Rachel Van Dyken** - With her "Eagle Elite" series, Van Dyken offers a gripping look at mafia life through the eyes of young adults. *Elite* and *Elect* are particularly noted for their intense romance and intricate plot twists.

• **Reilly Chase** - The "Hostile Operations Team" series, while more military romance, intersects with mafia elements, offering high-stakes action and complex relationships.

• **Sierra Simone** - Renowned for her darker, erotically charged narratives, Simone's "New Camelot" series, though not traditional mafia romance, intertwines elements of power, politics, and forbidden love that resonate with fans of the genre. Her ability to weave complex emotional stories with intense relationships makes her works a study in character depth and narrative tension.

• **Kresley Cole** - Best known for her paranormal romances, Cole's "The Professional" part of the "Game Maker" series, ventures into the mafia romance territory. It showcases her skill in creating alpha heroes and strong heroines, set against a backdrop of the Russian mafia. The series is noted for its steamy scenes, emotional depth, and thrilling plot.

• **J.J. McAvoy** - "Ruthless People" series is a compelling saga of two powerful mafia families coming together through marriage. McAvoy's storytelling is known for its ruthless characters, intricate plot lines, and a gripping narrative that explores the complexities of power and love within the mafia world.

• **Penelope Douglas** - Though primarily known for her new adult and dark romance works, Douglas's "Kill Switch," part of the "Devil's Night" series, blends elements of suspense, dark romance, and crime, offering readers intense psychological depth and twisted love stories that echo the themes found in mafia romance.

• **Tillie Cole** - Her "Scarred Souls" series delves into the darker corners of the criminal underworld, featuring characters that are both deeply scarred and incredibly resilient. Cole's work stands out for its emotional intensity, exploring themes of redemption, survival, and the healing power of love in the face of adversity.

• **Mariana Zapata** - Known for her slow-burn romances, Zapata's "Luna and the Lie" hints at the underworld ties and offers a nuanced exploration of relationships and personal growth. While not a mafia romance in the traditional sense, her ability to develop characters and relationships over time offers valuable insights into building tension and emotional investment.

• **Lisa Kleypas** - A veteran romance author, Kleypas's "Devil in Winter" from the "Wallflowers" series, while historically set, introduces readers to a protagonist with ties to the underworld, showcasing her skill in creating complex characters and emotionally charged narratives that can inspire mafia romance writers.

• **A. Zavarelli** - Known for her emotionally charged and gritty narratives, Zavarelli's "Boston Underworld" series is a standout in the genre. Books like *Crow* and *Reaper* offer readers a deep dive into the Irish mafia, featuring dark, brooding heroes and strong, resilient heroines caught in a web of danger, loyalty, and forbidden love.

• **B.B. Reid** - Reid brings a unique twist to the genre with her "Broken Love" series, blending elements of dark romance with the suspenseful underpinnings of the mafia world. Her ability to craft stories that are both dark and tantalizingly romantic has garnered a dedicated following.

• **L.J. Shen** - While Shen is widely recognized for her contemporary romances, her book *The Kiss Thief* stands out as a compelling foray into mafia romance. Shen's writing is known for its intense character dynamics, steamy scenes, and emotional depth, making her work a must-read for enthusiasts of the genre.

• **Sophie Lark** - Lark's "Brutal Birthright" series has quickly become a favorite among mafia romance readers. Her narratives, which include *Brutal Prince* and *Stolen Heir*, are celebrated for their intricate plots, complex characters, and the seamless blending of romance and suspense within the mafia context.

• **Meagan Brandy** - Brandy, primarily known for her new adult romances, ventures into the realm of mafia romance with *Fumbled Hearts*, a story that intertwines young love with the shadows of organized crime. Her engaging storytelling and character development offer a fresh perspective on the genre.

• **Natasha Knight** - Knight is a prolific author in the world of dark and mafia romance. Her "Benedetti Brothers" series, featuring titles like *Salvatore* and *Dominic*, dives into the heart of the mafia lifestyle, exploring themes of power, revenge, and love with a sharp, engaging narrative voice.

• **CD Reiss** - Offering a sophisticated take on the genre, Reiss's "Songs of Submission" series, though not strictly mafia, weaves elements of power, control, and danger in a way that resonates with fans of mafia romance. Her work is known for its lyrical prose and complex character psychology.

• **Giana Darling** - A standout author in the genre, Darling's "The Evolution of Sin" and "The Fallen Men" series delve into the dark and alluring aspects of forbidden love within the confines of the mafia world. *Lessons in Corruption* from "The Fallen Men" series is particularly notable for its exploration of love, power, and redemption.

• **Amo Jones** - Known for crafting dark and edgy romance, Jones's "The Elite Kings Club" series, though not traditional mafia, weaves elements of secrecy, power, and danger in a manner that resonates with fans of mafia romance. *The Silver Swan* is a compelling entry point into her intricate, suspenseful world.

• **Isabella Starling & Demi Donovan** - Collaborating on *Collateral*, Starling and Donovan plunge readers into a story of debt, revenge, and passion. Their combined storytelling brings a fresh, intense dynamic to the genre, making their work a must-read for those intrigued by the intersections of power and love.

• **T.M. Frazier** - Frazier's "King" series, while encompassing elements of dark romance and crime, shares thematic resonances with mafia romance through its exploration of survival, loyalty, and love in a lawless world. *King* and *Tyrant* are standout books that showcase her gritty, compelling narrative style.

• **Annika Martin** - Martin's "Dangerous Royals" series is renowned for its thrilling blend of action, suspense, and romance. *Dark Mafia Prince* introduces readers to a world where heritage, duty, and passion collide, offering a unique take on the mafia romance theme.

• **Cole McCade** - Though McCade's works often span various romance subgenres, his foray into darker themes with *Criminal Intentions* series brings a nuanced exploration of crime and passion that fans of mafia romance might find intriguing, blending procedural elements with deep character studies.

• **Skyla Madi** - Madi's "Syndicate" series offers a gripping look into organized crime, with *Your Heart for Mine* standing out as a poignant tale of love, sacrifice, and the lengths one will go to protect what is theirs in the dangerous world of the mafia.